The
Space Bug

The
Space Bug

Written by Nicola Matthews
Illustrated by Eleanor Taylor

Hooked On Phonics®

Hooked On Phonics®

Contents

Special Words

Special words help make this story fun.
Your child may need help reading them.

balcony

fountain

park

space

spaceship

under

wing

1. Can Polly Be Good?

Mom needs to go shopping. Max does not want to go with her, but he has to go. Mom wants him to find Polly, the dog, and put her in the truck.

"I cannot find her," says Max.

"Is she under the bed with the socks?" asks Mom.

Max looks under his bed.
No Polly!

"Did Polly go to get a drink?"
asks Mom.

Max looks, but no Polly.

"Is Polly by the TV?" asks Mom. "She likes to see the basketball games."

Max looks by the TV. No Polly.
"Well, I know she is here,"
says Mom. "Let's look out back."

Polly likes to dig and chase the cats.

Mom and Max go look in the back and in the shed, but Polly is not there.

They check the frogs too. Polly likes to chase the frogs. But she is not there.

"Well, we have to go now, or all the shops will be shut," says Mom. "I do not think Polly can come with us."

When Mom and Max get into the truck, Max says, "What is that sound?"

"What?" asks Mom.

"That dig, dig, dig sound!" says Max.

Mom gets out to look, and there, under the truck, is Polly. There is mud all over her.

She has just dug up the good
bone that she lost.

"Get in the truck, Polly!"
says Mom.

Polly hops into the truck.
She sits on Max's lap. She licks
his neck. She grabs his hat.

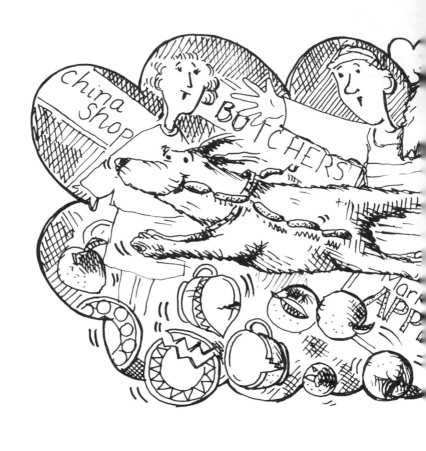

"Now, Polly," says Mom, "be a good dog in the shops. Do not run all over and smack into things.

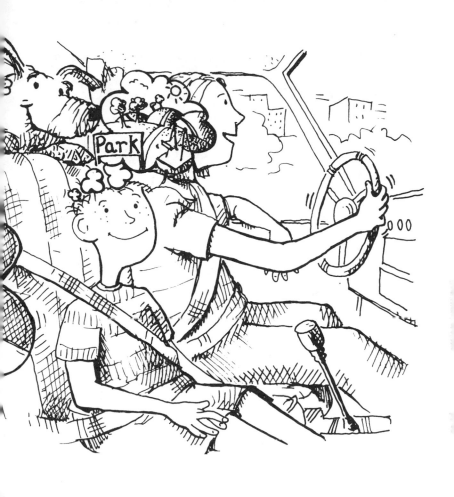

Do not grab snacks. Do not play
ball with things. Do not hop in the
fountain. Do not be a problem.

"Max, if you can get Polly to be good, you can go to the park."

"OK," says Max. "I can do it!"

Max likes to go to the park a lot! Max will do anything to go to the park.

2. The Spaceship

Mom and Max and Polly do not know this, but a spaceship has come down in town! Jazz the space kid is in the ship.

Jazz wants to go out and see this odd planet, but she cannot find her pet, Zug.

Zug is a space bug. Zug likes to do what he wants, and he will NOT do what Jazz tells him to do!

Jazz looks for Zug all over the ship.

Is he in the clock?

He likes to play with the space frogs and the space slugs that are in there. No, Zug's not in the clock.

Is he in the big cans?

Zug likes to snack on all the odd things in there. No, Zug is not there.

Is he in her bed?

Zug likes to peck holes in
her blankets. No, Zug is not in
her bed.

"Zug, I am off to get a look at
this planet," says Jazz, "but I
cannot find you, so I will go
without you."

When she gets out of the spaceship, there is a dig, dig, dig sound!

Jazz looks down, and there, under the spaceship, is Zug.

There is mud all over him. He has lots and lots of good slugs.

"Do you have to do that now?" Jazz says. "I want to see some shops on this planet. You can come too, but you have to be good.

"This book tells us what to do on this planet. But there are lots of things you cannot do, so I think you have to stay in the spaceship!"

FIG 3.2

Bug

Earth person

DO NOT LET YOUR PET RUN UP WALLS.
THIS SCARES PEOPLE **A LOT.**

"No way!" says Zug.
"OK, you can come, but
you have to sit on my back,"

says Jazz. "You will look like a
backpack."

So Zug hops onto Jazz's back.

He does not like it up there.
Jazz shuts the spaceship and
runs off to see the planet.

3. Dog Sees Bug!

Mom and Max stop to chat in all the shops. But Polly wants to run and play.

That's when Polly runs out of the shop. Max does not see her go.

Zug is fed up too. He wants to flap his wings and his legs.

He does not want to be a
backpack, so he hops off Jazz's
back. She does not see him skip off.
That's when Polly runs by.

She wants to have fun too.
  Zug looks like a good bug
to chase!

Now Zug wants to be good, but
he wants to have fun too.

Zug stops to look at all of the
things they have on this planet.

Zug sees a big dog run up to him!
"Oh, no! A big dog!" says Zug.

Zug sees steps that go up to a balcony. He runs up them. Polly runs up them too.

It's a trap! Zug wants to run from the dog, so he hops down from the balcony.

"Oh, no!" he yells.

But then he says, "I am a space bug! Space bugs have wings!"

Zug flaps his wings, and up he zips.

That's when Polly hops off the balcony to get Zug. But Polly is a dog.

SHOPS

FOUNTAIN

PARKING

Polly does not have wings!
"Woof!" she yells.
Mom and Max see Polly hop off
the balcony.

They run to get her. Mom looks
up at Polly. So does Max.

Mom runs smack into Max!
"Wooooooooooooof!" yells Polly.
Then she plops down on top
of them.

Polly is a big dog, and Mom and Max have to sit down.

But Polly does not stop. She is OK, so she runs to get that bug!

4. A Wet Mess

Mom and Max get up.

"Stop that dog!" yells Mom. She runs to get Polly.

"Here, Polly!" yells Max, and he runs to get Polly too. But Polly does not stop!

That's when Zug sees a
fountain. He thinks it looks like
lots of fun, so he hops in.

"This is fun!" he says with a big space bug grin. But Polly sees Zug, so she hops in the fountain too.

Polly is a big dog. She makes a big SPLAT! Zug gets all wet.

Zug swims off, but Polly grabs him!

Zug pecks Polly!

Then Zug flaps his big wet
wings and gets Polly all wet too.

"Stop this NOW!" yells Mom,
but the pets do not stop.

Mom gets into the fountain and
grabs Polly by the neck.

Max gets into the fountain to help Mom.

Moms, dads, kids, and dogs all stop to look at the mess.

They think it's fun to see a mom, a kid, a dog, and a space bug in the fountain.

"Polly!" says Mom. "What did you do?"

"Woof!" says Polly.

That's when Jazz finds Zug in the fountain too.

"What did you do, Zug?"
she says.
Then Jazz sees Mom and Max.

"I am Jazz, the space kid," she says. "This is Zug, my pet. I am sorry if he upset you."

"That's OK," Mom says. "Zug
and Polly are pets, and pets like
to have fun."

Mom and Max hug Jazz.
Then Max says, "Let's go to the
park where they can play."

And that's what they did. They all went to the park, and Polly ran with Zug, and Max and Jazz ran with the pets. They all had fun. And thanks to Jazz, Max got to go to the park after all!